Published in Great Britain in 2001 by Hodder Wayland, an imprint of
Hodder Children's Books

ISBN: 0 7502 3533 0

Designed by Leishman Design

Printed in Hong Kong by Wing King Tong

Hodder Children's Books
A division of Hodder Headline Limited
338 Euston Road, London NW1 3BH

Downhill Biker

MICHAEL HARDCASTLE

Illustrated by Dave Thompson

an imprint of Hodder Children's Books

Chapter One

There was no one in sight as Aaron aimed his bike at the narrow gap between two parked cars. He'd built up plenty of speed along the cobbled street and he wasn't going to slow down now. To his delight he shot between the cars as if they weren't there. "Just *knew* I could do it!" he said to himself.

Now, he swerved sharply past the supermarket entrance and into the deserted pedestrian precinct. He rode at top speed past a building society, then a baker's and into Castle Square. It felt wonderful to be freeriding in a place that was normally so crowded. For his next trick Aaron went into a controlled skid, cleverly sliding the bike all the way round one of the wide wooden seats lining the square. Close as he was, he never touched it.

Aaron punched the air, "Yes!" before turning his bike to do it again.

Then he heard a loud voice calling out: "Right lad, that's enough. Stop immediately!"

Aaron braked so hard that he almost dived over the handlebars. Then he swung round and saw a policeman standing in front of a shop window with his arms folded. "D'you mean me?" he called back.

The policeman made a pantomime of looking in every direction for someone else before barking: "Don't try funny games with me, lad. Of course I mean you! You're the only one breaking the laws of this town. This area is for pedestrians, not kids on mountain bikes. It says so on the sign up there. You can read, I suppose?"

Aaron closed his eyes. He felt like speeding off as fast as possible, but if he did that he'd be in real trouble. Instead, he said politely: "Yes, officer".

By now, the policeman was standing in front of him. "Look lad, I could book you for what you've just done, but I'm a kind fella so I won't. I'll just warn you: if I catch you riding in this precinct again I'll confiscate your bike. In case you don't understand that word, it means you'll lose it – for good. Got that?"

Aaron shrugged. "But I always ride my bike on the pavements when I deliver newspapers..." he started to say, but the policeman held up his hand like a traffic cop.

"You don't deliver them this late so forget that excuse," he said. "Speaking of which, your Mum and Dad must be wondering where you are. Now, get off home. And use the roads not the pavements."

Riding in a wide sweep, Aaron cycled slowly away from the precinct and aimed his bike for home. Before he'd gone even a hundred metres, however, another cyclist shot out of a side turning. He cut across in front of him, then skidded to a halt.

"Hey, you idiot!" Aaron shouted, startled. Then he recognised the other rider: Dean King from his class and his least favourite person. Dean was always full of himself, forever boasting about everything he did.

"You just got copped, didn't you?" Dean said, grinning. His feet were planted firmly on the road as he sat astride his bike blocking Aaron's way.

"No I didn't. He just gave me a sort of warning. Anyway how do you know?"

"I was watching from behind the arch by the library," Dean answered. "The cops would never catch *me*. I'm supersonic. This bike is the fastest thing on two wheels!"

Aaron found that hard to believe, but Dean's gleaming red and silver mountain bike was certainly impressive. It made his own machine look like something ready for the dump.

He wondered how Dean could afford such an expensive bike, but he wasn't going to ask. He knew Dean would only come up with another boastful story.

"Yeah, well, it's not how good the bike is, but how good the rider is!" Aaron declared, pleased with this reply. But he should have known better. Dean bounced right back with:

"Exactly! And I'm going to prove *I'm* the best when I win the Three Peaks Race! Nobody'll have a hope of catching me – certainly not you on that battered old junkpile. Everyone will watch me speed further and further into the lead."

Dean was talking about next week's school trip to Redville Camp in the Holden Hills. Everyone going for the four-day stay was in their year group. One of the highlights was going to be a downhill bike race. Anyone could compete and there were prizes for the first three places. It had been organized by Mrs Haining, one of the PE teachers and a keen mountain biker herself.

Aaron had never won a sports prize in his life, but he thought he might have a chance of winning this one. After all, he knew he was a pretty good rider. Although he'd never tested his speed, he was pretty confident that he was as fast as anyone. But would he be able to beat Dean on his gleaming new machine?

"I might have a new bike by then," was all Aaron could think of to say. He couldn't see how that would ever happen, but he wasn't going to let Dean treat him like some loser.

"It doesn't matter what you ride, you won't beat me," Dean insisted. "Remember, I'm King of the Mountains. I'm brilliant going uphill and I'm untouchable coming down. See you around – Ron!" Then he cycled away with a fierce burst of speed.

Aaron winced. He hated it when anyone shortened his name. But that wasn't what really bothered him. His mind was focussed on winning the Three Peaks Race, and he knew that he'd have to be super-fit to beat riders like Dean King.

Chapter Two

After school next day, Aaron set out for Scotland Park determined to do some serious training. A high mound called Signal Hill stood in the park. It had a smooth, winding path spiralling down from the top in a series of very tight turns, with one section that was a set of steep steps. At the top stood the statue of an old war hero. Aaron knew the only people who ever went up there were a few joggers testing their stamina. So, with luck, no one would see him if he biked down it at top speed. He'd be *really* unlucky to meet another policeman!

It was a real slog to get to the top, even using the gears. The slope was much steeper than he'd remembered. It was only the thought of the downhill ride that kept him going. "I'm glad nobody's watching," he panted. "They'd think I was about as fit as a mashed potato."

The downhill start was fast and in seconds Aaron was speeding... *really* speeding. There were moments when he was desperate to yank on the brakes, but he knew that could be dangerous. Downhill rides were all about taking risks, about daring to do frightening things. And it was those risks that gave you a buzz when you were riding to win.

The biggest risk of all was the flight of steps: he would have to jump them. Aaron licked his dry lips and felt his heart thumping. But it didn't enter his head to slow down, let alone stop and walk down the steps one by one. He knew the slope he would land on was gentle and wouldn't catapult him into the air again. Tight round another sharp bend, a slight touch on the brakes, the steps coming up, pedalling hard and then... lift off!

For a few moments Aaron was airborne. Fantastic! But he still remembered to lean back over the rear wheel for landing. To land front wheel first might mean disaster.

Down! The back wheel touched the ground and gave a momentary wobble. Nothing worse. He'd done it – he'd jumped the steps! Now the biggest risk of all on Signal Hill was behind him.

As he flashed round one of the wider turns near the foot of the hill, Aaron thought he glimpsed someone watching him. It didn't matter who'd seen him anyway, because he felt on top of the world. He decided it had been the best ride of his life. Taking off his cycle helmet, he let out a big, happy sigh. Then he lay his bike down and sank back against a tree trunk.

Moments later, another cyclist glided down the path and stopped suddenly beside him. Aaron jumped to his feet in alarm and then saw that it was Matt Sands, Dean's best friend.

"Trying to set a land-speed record, were you?" inquired Matt.

Matt laid his own bike down and inspected Aaron's old hardtail.

"Can't believe an antique like this could go so fast," he murmured, pulling at the spokes and prodding at the tyres. "Could be dangerous to go the speed you were doing."

"It's fine, it'd go even faster if I needed it to," Aaron replied, wishing he knew what Matt was up to.

"No, no that could be really dangerous," Matt said, shaking his head slowly. "If it collapses in a race you'd come off and you might bring down other riders. That would cause a real problem. We can't allow that – Ronnie!"

Then Matt picked up the bike, pushed it quickly across the path and heaved it over a low stone wall.

Aaron had been slow to guess Matt's plan, so hadn't even tried to stop him. Now he dashed across to the wall and gazed down in horror at his bike. It had crash-landed onto a flagstone patio below. He could see it was still in one piece but couldn't tell how bad the damage was.

"You scum! You rotten scum, Sands!" Aaron stormed.

"You shouldn't yell at me, you should thank me," was the calm reply. "I've saved you from a nasty fall. You'll thank me one day, Ronnie."

Then Matt rode away laughing.

Aaron raced down a flight of steps to the patio to examine his precious bike. The frame was bent just in front of the saddle and the front fork was wonky.

To his surprise, the wheels looked okay. But, as soon as he tried to ride it, he knew the damage was bad. The bike felt as if it might collapse in a heap at any moment.

Somehow, though, he got home. He rode it part of the way and pushed it the rest, all the time thinking about Matt. He wished he'd thumped him, although he knew that wouldn't have solved anything. One day, he thought grimly, he'd find the perfect way to get his revenge.

Chapter Three

At school next day, Aaron avoided contact with Matt and Dean but they didn't try to speak to him either. Whenever they saw him, they just exchanged satisfied smiles.

Aaron asked everyone he could think of to lend him a bike for the school trip to Redville Camp. He pleaded, promising money and huge favours, but it was hopeless. No one could help him. Nobody had a spare bike and nobody wanted to be separated from their own bike for almost a week.

However, at breakfast next morning, Aaron found an answer. His dad mentioned that he'd have to get the car serviced shortly and that reminded Aaron of Mac, the mechanic his dad used. Well, if Mac could repair a car he would surely be able to deal with a bike.

As soon as school was over, Aaron dashed across town to Mac's Motors in Pipe Street to ask for help. "I can pay," Aaron said, crossing his fingers that the bill would be low. Mac, however, said that while money didn't worry him, metal bashing did. It wasn't his thing. "I give that work to another bloke," he explained. "I could send it to him for you but he's got loads on at the moment, so you won't get the bike back for, oh, three weeks earliest."

"That's no good," Aaron said, adding that the school trip was on Monday. "I'm desperate, Mac. Please, please do something for me."

Mac rubbed his chin and pushed his fingers through his hair and said "Well" and "I don't know" until, at last, he gave in. "I'll have a go, Aaron, but only because your dad's a good customer. Don't expect anything special. I might make a right botch of it."

"No you won't," Aaron told him confidently.

When he collected it next evening, however, Aaron's heart sank. His bike looked no better. "Sorry, Aaron, but I did warn you," Mac told him. "I didn't have much time and I'm afraid I couldn't do what was needed. Sorry, mate, but it needs an expert. No, no, there's no charge. I don't take payment for work I can't do."

As he rode away, Aaron thought the bike was moving better, even though it still looked battered. Then when he was almost home, it started a wheel wobble. He jumped off and inspected the wheels and frame closely. He couldn't see what was wrong, but he knew then that his chance of winning the Three Peaks Race was zero.

Chapter Four

"You're very quiet, Aaron," said Mrs Haining as the bus began its steep climb up a narrow road between two hills. "Don't tell me you're not looking forward to this school trip. I mean, it'll be more like a holiday."

"Yes, Miss, I'm sure it will," he replied politely. "I was, er, just thinking about the race."

"Is there a problem with it?" the teacher went on.

Aaron wasn't sure how much to tell her. "It's just, well, my bike has had a bit of an accident. I'm not sure that it'll be very good on steep hills like these," he admitted.

"Oh, I'm sure we'll be able to find someone to sort it out for you," she beamed. "I know Dean's a bit of an expert on the subject of bikes. Maybe we'll ask him to have a look. All right, Aaron?"

Aaron couldn't stop himself from glancing across at Dean. He was sitting on the opposite side of the aisle. Dean, of course, was grinning idiotically, and soon whispering to the giggling Matt. Aaron had to swallow hard to prevent

himself saying what he really thought of Dean's expertise with bikes. If he had, then the school trip would be finished for him before it had really started. He managed the mildest response: "Thanks, Miss."

He looked so glum that a girl called Laura leant over and said: "Cheer up, Aaron. It may never happen."

"What may never happen?" he asked, puzzled.

"Your worst fears," she told him, smiling.

He tried to smile back but couldn't quite manage it. He liked Laura. She was all right, not like some of the silly, giggling girls he knew.

Then Will, Aaron's friend, piped up: "We'll think of something, Aaron, don't worry. There's bound to be somebody who's good at fixing things." But that just started Dean and Matt laughing again.

The amazing views from Redville Camp made Aaron cheer up. It was like being on top of the world. Wherever he looked there were high peaks that reached into the clouds. Thick bands of trees covered the slopes and a distant river wound through the valley. Aaron had never been anywhere so high in his life and he wondered what it would be like to live in such a brilliant place.

"Is that the bike track?" Will suddenly asked. "Over there, that sort of mini gap between those trees?"

Everyone looked in the direction he was pointing. Mrs Haining took out her binoculars and studied the scene while everyone else waited breathlessly.

"Yes, I'm sure it is," she agreed. "I expect that's the steepest part, too, because there's quite a drop down there."

"Oh great!" exclaimed Dean. "I'll be the BEST going down there! Nobody'll be able to catch me!"

Nobody else said anything until they reached the huts where they were staying. "Looks like a military camp," said Matt, who never missed a chance of telling everyone that he was going to join the army one day.

The two long, low huts were raised up on brick pillars to keep them off the ground. The

boys were staying in one hut and the girls in the other. When they'd all unpacked their gear, Mr Coledale said that everyone needed exercise. "We'll have a game of volleyball," he said. "With boys and girls on the same teams, before anyone gets any other ideas. Should be good fun! When you play this high up you're on top form!"

Dean moaned: "We should be riding our bikes, sir, getting ourselves ready for the race not bashing some old ball about."

"Plenty of time for that later, Dean," smiled Mr Coledale. "Volleyball will exercise your arm as well as your leg muscles."

Aaron wasn't mad about ball games but he didn't mind them. He quite liked the idea of scoring goals and jumping high to smash a ball over the net with his fist.

Mrs Haining chose the teams. There were the usual grumbles from people who'd ended up on the

opposite team to their friends. Aaron was pleased that he was on the orange team, though, because Laura was too.

Dean was on the green team. It wasn't long before he tried to show off. When the ball came towards him he jumped and tried a fierce punch, missing it completely. What was worse, as he landed on the uneven ground he lost his balance and sat down with a bump. Aaron wasn't the only one who laughed – even Mrs Haining was grinning – but it was Aaron who got a blazing scowl from Dean.

Moments later, it was Aaron's turn to leap and try a punch from close to the net. His timing was perfect – hitting the ball with all of his strength over the net sent it flying down. Not even a pro player could have saved it from smacking the ground and scoring a goal.

"Well done, Aaron, really well hit," Mr Coledale called out. This time Matt sent a fierce scowl too. But Aaron didn't care. Suddenly, he was enjoying himself and happy they'd all come to Redville Camp.

The game continued with the orange team a goal up. Then, just before the end, Aaron was in the right spot to palm the ball up towards Laura. He yelled: "Go on, Laura! Shoot!" And she did, leaping high to bang the ball downwards over the net with her fists.

"Yes!" she shouted as she scored the second goal. Then she turned and sent a big smile in Aaron's direction. Two minutes later the game ended with the oranges as the winners. They were all supposed to shake hands politely, but Matt tried to crush Aaron's hand while Dean avoided him completely.

"You OK, Will?" said Aaron as he turned to shake his hand. "You look awful!" Will felt awful. He'd fallen over during the game and then someone had landed on his left foot. Mrs Haining helped him to a seat and went off to get some ice to stop the swelling.

It had been a long day. After the evening meal most people were tired and stayed indoors talking or playing games. Aaron decided to have a last look at his bike before bed time. It had been stored on a trailer with everyone else's. Only when he got there, his bike had vanished! Aaron checked and double-checked, but his bike was definitely missing.

He had no doubt who'd taken it. "Where've you put it?" he demanded when he found Dean. Of course, Dean was with Matt and they didn't even try denying they were responsible. They just exchanged winks and loud laughs.

"Come on, you've stolen it," Aaron pointed out angrily. "People get into big trouble for thieving."

"You should watch your property," Matt said. "Very careless of you to lose it. But that's because you're thinking of GIRLS all the time."

Aaron blinked. "Girls? I don't know what you're on about."

They laughed. "Well ask them. Maybe girls UNDERstand you. Get it? UNDERstand."

It took Aaron a few moments to work it out. His bike must be under the girls' hut, a place he'd never have thought of looking. He dashed over to it and asked Alice Greene, the first girl he saw, if she'd seen anything suspicious going on. Alice said she'd seen Matt scrambling about near their hut earlier on. He had claimed he was looking for a lost ball.

Aaron dropped to his knees and peered into the gloom beneath the hut. He thought he could just make out a glint of metal but he couldn't be sure. What he needed was a torch but he'd no idea how to get hold of one. In any case, the teachers were rounding everyone up and telling them to go to bed immediately. Aaron decided the only thing he could do was to carry out his search in the middle of the night.

A couple of hours later he was sure everyone was asleep. He didn't think he could keep awake much longer himself. Armed with a borrowed cycle lamp, he crept across the narrow space between the huts. There wasn't a sound and no sign of anyone. But he trembled with worry in case he was spotted.

Under the hut there was just enough room for him to move about without banging his head. At one point he froze – he could hear whispering voices above him. He guessed that a couple of girls couldn't sleep. It meant he had to be more careful than ever not to make a noise.

At last he could almost touch his bike. It was impossible to tell whether it was now even more damaged but he'd find out when he'd pulled it out. But, as soon as he started to pull the bike there was a scraping sound. He froze again.

Had anybody heard the sound? What about the girls just above? He waited for as long as he could and then again started to drag out the bike. This time he managed it without making any more noise. His mouth was so dry he would have given anything for a drink.

Aaron had just backed out from under the hut and was getting to his feet when a beam of light shone directly into his eyes. "Stop there, Aaron!" a familiar voice said angrily.

"What do you think you're up to? Trying to scare the girls, was that it?"

"No sir, honestly!" Aaron was shocked that Mr Coledale should think he would do anything so mean.

"Of course you were. Couldn't possibly be any other reason for creeping under their hut in the middle of the night. I'm ashamed of you, Aaron, really ashamed."

"But I was getting my bike, sir. This one. Look, it is mine. Somebody had hidden it under there."

"Huh," Mr Coledale snorted, "a likely excuse. Well, you've got some imagination, I'll say that for you. Off to bed with you, now! We'll deal with this in the morning. But you don't need me to tell you that you're in deep, deep trouble. Now, come on, back to the boys' hut!"

Aaron swallowed hard. "Can I put my cycle away first, please? I mean – "

"You leave it where it is. I'll deal with it. Anyway, you won't be riding it again in a hurry."

Aaron had no choice but to do as he was told. Slowly he made his way back to the boys' hut and climbed into bed. He didn't think he could possibly sleep after such a dreadful experience but he did. He was totally exhausted. Before dropping off, his mind focussed on one thing: his bike. For even as Mr Coledale was going on at him, Aaron had seen that the front wheel was no longer round. It had been bent completely out of shape. Mr Coledale's words were true, he wouldn't be riding that bike again for a while.

Chapter Five

It was Laura who got him out of trouble. For, of course, the story of the night's adventures had spread like a forest fire. Everyone was talking about it. Then Alice told everyone about Matt and the lost ball and Aaron asking her if she'd seen anything suspicious. When she heard this, Laura dashed off to find Mr Coledale and tell him that Aaron's story was true. Someone else really had stashed his bike away under the hut.

"Well, I must say, it all did seem out of character for Aaron," Mrs Haining admitted.

"And he'd hardly shove his own bike under the hut, especially as it's unrideable now. I think we'd better have a word with Dean and Matt. Always as thick as thieves, those two."

Of course, both boys flatly denied having anything to do with the bike-under-the-hut mystery. Matt even produced a battered tennis ball to show the teachers. "Look, that's the ball I lost. I found it under *our* hut, the boys' hut." The boys had heard all the rumours about the investigation so their answers were carefully prepared. Hard as he tried, Mr Coledale couldn't

shake Matt and Dean's confidence in their story. In the end he had to accept it, even though he still suspected they were the guilty ones. He needed, though, to have another word with the original suspect – Aaron.

"You acted stupidly, Aaron," he told him. "But I believe you were telling the truth. In part, at least, you can thank Laura. She's obviously a loyal friend. Anyway, I don't want you wandering about again in the middle  of the night. If you'd got stuck under that hut there could have been all sorts of trouble. Lucky for you, I was up and about because I thought I heard a prowler. Right, we'll do our best to forget this incident but be warned, Aaron, don't do anything so silly again."

By now Aaron could think only of his battered bike. "How am I going to ride in the Three Peaks Race, sir? My bike's useless."

Mr Coledale looked genuinely sorry. "Well, Aaron I don't think we can do anything about that. I mean, we didn't bring any spare bikes with us and there's nobody able to repair your machine, even if it *can* be repaired. Sorry. We'll try and think of something."

In his heart, Aaron knew they wouldn't be able to help him. He was out of the race before he even had a chance of winning it. If he could find some way of getting his revenge on Dean and Matt, he would.

A few minutes later, Laura found him sitting on a log overlooking the steepest valley.

"Hey, you're not looking miserable again, are you?" she greeted him. "I thought you'd be smiling again now you're out of trouble."

He looked up, startled. "Oh, hi. Don't know what you mean by being *out* of trouble. I mean, I still haven't got a bike I can ride. So I've no chance of winning the race, have I? What's that if it's not trouble?"

Laura frowned, thinking hard. Then she said: "Got it! Why don't you borrow a bike? Will's a good mate, isn't he? And he won't be able to ride his bike after that injury to his foot. So why don't we ask him?"

Aaron blinked in surprise. Why hadn't he thought of that? "But why would Will lend anyone such a good bike? I mean, a bike's a very personal possession, isn't it?" he said.

Laura jumped to her feet. "Only way to find out, Aaron, is to ask. Come on."

When they found him, Will was actually polishing the already gleaming blue and yellow frame of his full-suspension mountain bike. His foot was still bandaged and he was limping.

"Aaron's got a favour to ask you, Will," said Laura, getting straight to the point.

Aaron thought he might as well follow Laura's direct approach: "Will, if you can't ride in the race, will you lend me your bike?" he pleaded. "I mean, it would be a waste if a bike as good as yours wasn't competing, wouldn't it?"

For a few moments, Will didn't reply. It was plain from his expression that he didn't really know what to say. Aaron decided he needed to make a promise. "Look, Will, I'll treat it just like my own. I won't take any risks that might damage it or anything. And if I win and there's any prize money, you can have half of it – no, all of it!"

Will managed a small, wan smile. "No mate, I don't want your money – *if* you win it. But I suppose you're right about the bike. I would like to show it off because it's the best bike here by miles. So, OK, you can ride it. But, remember it's valuable. So don't bash it about whatever you do."

Aaron was amazed that he'd got what he wanted so easily. "Thanks, Will, you're a real friend," he said, slapping him on the back. "If there's anything I can ever do for you, just ask."

Moments later, Aaron was on the bike, turning in tight circles and making wide sweeps. He would have liked to ride the bike down a steep bank to check the suspension and the braking system, but he sensed that the watching Will wouldn't have felt too happy about it, especially if it skidded out of control or something. This was why he didn't do a victory wheelie, either, before giving his verdict.

"Will, it's fantastic! You're a mega star to let me borrow it."

Will didn't say anything, but managed a slightly warmer smile.

"Thanks, Laura, you were a great help," Aaron told her when they were on their own again.

"Well, just make
sure you *do* win because that'll really put the
skids under Dean," she replied. "Everyone here
must be sick to death of his non-stop boasting
by now."

It didn't take long for the others to hear about
the loan of Will's brand-new, full-sus bike. Dean
and Matt immediately went into a huddle. They
sat well away from the rest and began to hatch a
plot to stop Aaron. Although he didn't want to
admit it, Dean knew that Aaron was a real threat
to his own chances of winning the race. And
winning the Three Peaks was Dean's greatest
ambition. It would prove that he truly was King
of the Mountains. But what he and Matt needed
to know first was what the route was like.

They didn't have to wait long. That afternoon, Mrs Haining led everybody around the course.

It was a clear day with pale sunshine although there were some dark clouds in the far distance. "I know this looks like a good day for a race but that's not until tomorrow," Mrs Haining told them. "So *nobody* is to start racing on this circuit today. This is just a recce. You're here to find out what you'll be facing tomorrow. We'll be looking at the narrow bits, the steep bits, the dangerous bits – because there are some, I promise – we'll be looking at where you can speed up but also where total care is vital. Got that?"

Aaron was surprised how narrow the track became after the early descent. It was often impossible for two people to ride side by side.

Perhaps the most scenic bit of the route was a wooden bridge over a fast-flowing stream. It came after a sharp left-hander and then immediately swung to the right. Not only was the bridge in the middle of an "S", it was well screened by trees growing out of the slopes at different angles.

Most people were out of breath by the time they returned to the camp. "I don't think I'll ever get as far as this tomorrow," Laura gasped when they all collapsed on reaching the top.

"Course you will," Aaron said, grinning.

Chapter Six

That night it took Aaron ages to get to sleep. He thought he would be exhausted after last night's adventures and the course recce. Yet, as he thought about his tactics for the next day, he found it hard to drop off. He'd worked out exactly what he must do. He wasn't going to change his mind.

Dean and Matt were on the other side of the room. They were whispering to each other as usual. It worried Aaron that they might try to sabotage Will's bike. However, he knew Mr Coledale had already thought of that and had locked away all the bikes as well as everyone's protective gear.

Next morning after breakfast it started to rain. Visibility was still good so no one worried about the race, apart from Mrs Haining. "The rain may make parts of the track slippery," she warned them as they lined up for the start.

"I know you all want to go at top speed but you've got to take care. We've got marshals posted at various points and if they see anyone going too fast, or acting stupidly, they'll pull him or her out of the race. So, remember – watch your speed!"

Aaron, listening carefully, grinned at Laura. She could guess that he was thinking about *his* speed and how his plans might work out. He'd told her how much the race meant to him.

Aaron looked across at his enemies, Dean and Matt, who were side by side and talking away. Then he smiled at Will. "Thanks again for the bike, Will. It feels even better today. As if I'm part of it, or it's part of me."

Before Will could answer, the race was on. And his bike sped away first as Aaron made an absolutely flying start.

He'd worked out that he needed to avoid the early crush. If he was ahead of the rest then he couldn't run into trouble if other people got in his way. Nor would he have to weave his way through a crowd of slow riders. If he set the pace, other people would have to change any plans they'd made but he'd be able to stick with his.

Aaron felt no fears whatsoever when riding downhill, however steep. It was what he loved. But some of the marshals were worried by the pace he was setting. "Slow down!" they warned him. "You're going too fast!" He knew he wasn't, that he could handle speed, but he waved to show them he'd heard.

Everyone else was surprised by Aaron's storming start. Dean and Matt caught a fleeting glimpse of the flying leader far below them as they made a sweeping turn on an easy bend. Dean gulped. He knew he couldn't let his rival get too far ahead, though he was confident he would out-ride him on the uphill sections.

"We've got to stop him," he shouted to Matt.

"Yeah, but how?" Matt wanted to know.

"We'll use the plan," Dean decided.

"Now?" Matt asked, surprised.

"Now!"

So Matt broke away from the pack. He waited until he was sure he couldn't be seen and then, half-carrying, half-pushing his bike, he cut through the crowded trees and bushes at the side of the track. He made his way as fast as he could down the uneven slopes to the lower level near the wooden bridge. If he was lucky, no one would see him hiding there. On the recce, he and Dean had spotted it as the ideal place for an ambush. But they'd reckoned that Aaron would be behind them when the race reached that point. If he was ahead, then that would make the attack easier still.

With no idea of what was coming, Aaron sped on. He was having a terrific time riding Will's amazing bike. Its double shocks and the light V-brakes made sure that he felt totally in control, however hazardous the track – and the rain was certainly affecting the ground in places. In fact, the bike was perfect for a race like this. He was thankful he'd spent some time the night before getting used to it. All the same, he thought it wise to slow down when another marshal warned him that he was overdoing it. At this stage, the marshals would be likely to disqualify riders who didn't listen.

Aaron had built up a big lead by the time he reached the wooden bridge. Here, the change of surface slowed him down a little. This pause saved him from disaster, because Matt suddenly charged out of the trees, aiming his bike straight at him.

"This is the end of the race for you, Ronnie!" he yelled.

Aaron reacted instantaneously. As Matt hurtled towards him, Aaron whipped his bike sideways and then pulled back in a half-circle.

The manoeuvre was too quick for Matt. He tried to brake but his tyres wouldn't grip on the rain-slicked wooden bridge. He was still sliding and unable to stop as the track swung sharply to the right. Helplessly, he plunged down a steep slope and crashed straight into a thick clump of gorse bushes.

"Revenge!" Aaron cried. "And I never even touched him!"

Even before the next rider reached the bridge, Aaron was building up his lead again. He knew now that he was going to win the Three Peaks Race.

His enemies must have felt the only way of stopping him was literally to knock him out of the race. Well, they'd failed. His best revenge on Dean would be to beat him out of sight.

As he started the long, last climb there was still no one close behind him. The rider who called himself King of the Mountains had failed to live up to his name!

"Go on, son, you're winning by a mile!" a marshall yelled as Aaron caught sight of the camp a few hundred metres away. He was beginning to feel tired now, but he didn't slow down. He wanted to end the race as he had begun it, with a real burst of speed.

"Yes!" he yelled, punching the air with both fists as he rode over the finishing line to the sound of applause. Will was in the crowd, clapping madly and telling everyone that it was his bike that had come first.

The first girl home was Laura and, even better, she finished well ahead of Dean who told everyone that his bike had had a puncture. Matt didn't turn up until much later on. His ruined bike was battered from its slide into the bushes and his face and hands were badly scratched. He said that he'd skidded on a wet patch of ground.

"I never thought anyone could win as easily as you did," Mrs Haining said as she handed Aaron a silver cup. "Were you as confident as you looked, Aaron?"

"I was, Miss," he smiled. "I was riding the best bike in the race. Oh, and remember, there's a double-A at the start of my name. So I always expect to come first!"

Read more of Michael Hardcastle's sports stories:

INJURY TIME
Joe would be a really good player, if he weren't so accident prone. He always seems to be suffering from aches and pains and rarely gets through a match without injury. The coach thinks that he's a fake, but Amy's not sure. Could there be another reason for Joe's problem?

STRIKER'S BOOTS
Sean has waited for weeks to get a place on the school soccer team. He's almost given up hope when the coach picks him at last! Then disaster strikes. He's forgotten his boots. This could be Sean's big chance, but how can he score goals in bare feet?

SOCCER SECRET
Tom is a brilliant striker and he loves boasting about all the goals he scores. But he doesn't know that his cousin Alan is good at football too – as a goalie. Will Alan get the recognition he deserves, without upsetting Tom?

RIVALS UNITED
When East End's star striker defects to the West End team, his team-mates can't believe it. Just what does David think he's playing at? Then there's a local derby when the two teams meet. The winning team could be promoted to league status, but where do David's loyalties lie?

SKATEBOARD SECRET

When Robbie joins the skateboard gang he feels he's made a big mistake. First, his favourite skateboard mysteriously disappears and when builders demolish the gang's skatepark, Robbie gets the blame! Can the gang find somewhere else to skate? Will Robbie's board turn up? And what's behind Leo's grudge against him?

For more information about Mega Stars, please contact:
The Sales Department, Hodder Children's Books,
338 Euston Road, London NW1 3BH